For My Mom La W

With much love +
Gratitude for your friendship.

Michael *
5/13/92

* On Birthday!

THE NATIONAL POETRY SERIES

The National Poetry Series was established in 1978 to ensure the publication of five books of poetry each year through a series of participating publishers. Each manuscript is selected by a poet of national reputation. Publication is funded by the Copernicus Society of America, James A. Michener, Edward J. Piszek, and The Lannan Foundation.

1990 PUBLICATIONS

Words For My Daughter by John Balaban
Selected by W. S. Merwin. Copper Canyon Press.

Questions About Angels by Billy Collins
Selected by Edward Hirsch. William Morrow & Co.

The Island Itself by Roger Fanning
Selected by Michael Ryan. Viking Penguin.

Rainbow Remnants in Rock Bottom Ghetto Sky by Thylias Moss
Selected by Charles Simic. Persea Books.

The Surface by Laura Mullen
Selected by C. K. Williams. University of Illinois Press.

THE ISLAND ITSELF

THE ISLAND ITSELF

Roger Fanning

VIKING

VIKING

Published by the Penguin Group

Viking Penguin, a division of Penguin Books USA Inc.,
375 Hudson Street, New York, New York 10014, U.S.A.
Penguin Books Ltd, 27 Wrights Lane, London W8 5TZ, England
Penguin Books Australia Ltd, Ringwood, Victoria, Australia
Penguin Books Canada Ltd, 10 Alcorn Avenue, Suite 300,
Toronto, Ontario, Canada M4V 3B2
Penguin Books (N.Z.) Ltd, 182–190 Wairau Road, Auckland 10, New Zealand

Penguin Books Ltd, Registered Offices:
Harmondsworth, Middlesex, England

First published in 1991 by Viking Penguin,
a division of Penguin Books USA Inc.

10 9 8 7 6 5 4 3 2 1

Page v is an extension of this copyright page.

LIBRARY OF CONGRESS CATALOGING IN PUBLICATION DATA
Fanning, Roger.
The island itself/Roger Fanning.   p.   cm.
ISBN 0-670-84138-2
I. Title.
PS3556.A49I74   1991
811'.54—dc20   91–50243

Printed in the United States of America
Set in Fairfield Medium   Designed by Jessica Shatan

ACKNOWLEDGMENTS

Grateful acknowledgment is made to the editors of the following publications where these poems first appeared:

JEOPARDY:
"House on Fire"

QUAINT CANOE:
"Welcome to Big Wyoming"

THE SEATTLE REVIEW:
"Autobiographical"
"A Walk between Eleven and Twelve O'Clock"
"Goodwill Swirls Up in Thumbpools"
"The Sorrow of Underwear"
"Under a Turquoise Porch Light"

THE THREEPENNY REVIEW:
"Beyond the Cloud People"

THE VIRGINIA QUARTERLY REVIEW:
"Duckert the Effeminate, Zephyrlike Surgeon"
"Frog"
"Galapagos Islands, Guillotine Eyelids"
"Hospital Sidewalk"
"My Mother's Mouth"
"Story"

"Skagit Valley, 1980" and "Glint of Gold Tooth in a Poorly Lit Kitchen" originally appeared in THE NEW YORKER.

CONTENTS

THE ISLAND ITSELF

THE SORROW OF UNDERWEAR

From a side lane soft with lunar mulch
and thistledown I saw them, clipped alone
on a clothesline, a pair of diaphanous panties
as wide as an elephant's forehead.
I sighed across the boy-mown lawn
and they shook as though they shed blessings
to the moon and her tongue-tied exiles.
Who would dare pour such panties
along his arms and throat? A murderer, maybe.
The Milky Way was pavement
compared to their luxury. I knew
I wouldn't outwalk their whispers that night.

Next morning my feet felt like mallets.
I was back in the world where people
wear out, embarrassed by beautiful things,
and a garment fit for a goddess is nothing but big.

1

A WALK BETWEEN ELEVEN AND TWELVE O'CLOCK

I'd like to be unique yet clear, like
a snowflake straight into electric light.
But tonight, ninety degrees in an Iowa town, I'm viscous
and goat-giddy because elm leaves encase
with their jitters a streetlight. I can see
through the leaves, nearly, through the heated
white-green wave that hurls itself
toward the two moons of Mars but remains
a block from a mailbox. I look at it:
trunkbound bulk unlike a crystal ball.
I cannot see beyond leaves' veins—glyphic,
distinct—but I feel as though my iris flecks
and muscle flakes all fly to cool destinations.

The insects in this civic park sound crazy,
like mad ratchets or whirligig fireworks, like
rattlesnakes in the grip of their first religion.
Who and what will I outlive? There's more here
than one body's rocket ride and one hope
for more life. Stock-still I am rushing as a leaf
or pebble rushes. I am rushing with a pebble
in my pocket, through blackness and heat—even the insects
(unriveted) rush—driven clairvoyant by our lack of beliefs.

AUTOBIOGRAPHICAL

I had a childhood as moist and tangled
as the work clothes on my brother's bed.
I had the shadows of venetian blinds
to suggest where babies come from
and a poster of a palomino
that rose and fell near a table fan.
I saw a shambler, his gullet a swamp
of arms and legs, in the wood grain of my door.

Enough about me for now.
Everyone had a room with certain things
and certain nothings, wherever he and his parents
and the clubfooted angels thought they should be.

In a basement somewhere a civil servant

There a shirtless dwarf tilts ten cauldrons
of liquid gold, and brass. Pours it
into trophy shapes and molds for medals.
Grungy wet he shines gray, like a catfish

surfacing. Later on he shines less:
cutting out squares of lambskin
from little carcasses, for diplomas.
He labors all night. One day a week

a deaf young man lugs off the junk
we will covet, our names emblazoned.
Why must achievements be made official?
In a bad sleep the dwarf grinds green molars.

BEYOND THE CLOUD PEOPLE

By cloud people I mean elderly women
whose white hair poofs out: cumulocirrus.
Between the filaments blue ether flows.
It would be peaceful to lean my face in. . . .

Why don't I? After all, it's okay to touch
a pregnant woman, an acquaintance, where she feels
the baby move; I feel it too. We love
the unborn because we love the ideal

of a safe place where even as adults
we can, as over a campfire, warm our hands.

But a cloud hairdo looks cool, cold
as a person's last pillow. Oblivion we solo.

THE BIRTH OF ANTAEUS

My third grade class decided to plant
a Christmas cactus in a clay pot. Mrs. Fry picked me,
her spelling champ, to get the dirt.
She handed me a chartreuse bucket
and the magic trowel. My best friend clapped.

I skulked across the playground. Dust cycloned
into six foot fangs under the monkey bars
and haints whickered the swing set chains.
I knelt at the edge of the field
by the drainage ditch and poplars

and tore into the dirt. (I felt the same joy
years later in an air-conditioned,
all-night theater. The film
was in Spanish. I didn't understand
Spanish.) Then the bucket

was joggling at the end of my arm
as I tromped back, my eyes fixed
on B wing. Someone had pounded erasers
on the bricks, all the yellow chalk bangs
exclamation marks.

THE QUAIL EGG ORCHARD
· ·

Fifty yards down the cool slope the roots
of the squat quail egg trees
clutch flatland
and quail eggs hang by filaments
from the indigo branches.
I'm on my belly, up the slope
with a Benjamin air rifle
and aiming down the moonlight.
The first pellet splucks an egg.

All night I shoot. The yolks, whites, and blood
gurgle among the trunks, slide
like lava. In the scaly night heat
an embryo forms,
thousand-winged, soft-beaked, heart
as big as a pony keg.
The quail thing thumps to its feet, squalls
prehistoric, and flaps

over my head to terrify
the high school boy and girl
joined like earthworms
in a pickup truck with Kansas plates.

DANCE MANIAS DURING THE PLAGUE

Trying perhaps to stomp on some plague rats,
a few despairing folks would start to dance.
The Black Death thus had a fine side effect:
it brought people together. Their skulls bobbed
like opaque lanterns: brighter, brighter. Fear departed
in the form of crows. Soon, more limbs flailed

in street and field: hundreds tarantellaed.
Hollering dryhumpers also did cartwheels, and
at their hottest, the core of the crowd,
kissed visions of God. There was not one
wallflower. Hilarity, fistfights, animal snorts
and many fell down—it's fun to convulse—

till a chill picked apart their fervor
with tiny fingernails, tiny teeth. Most people
drifted home, nerves unknotted, relieved.
Others felt worse. A few, hearts burst
like toads thrown against a wall, gurgled:
gone. By increments, their chillbumps sank back in.

Then the moon rose to smooth all skin.
Are these tableaux eerie, or too familiar? Fanatics
dead in wet rags, and children with tremors
from this night forward, befogged and blotchy,
and especially grown-ups who just wanted a good time,
then nursed at soupbones in separate hovels.

CHRISTIAN'S AUTO WRECKING

Dad goes in and asks Bob Christian, Jr.,
if we can dump a freezer in his steelyard.
I wait in the truck
and note the guinea hens, peacocks, white geese.
They make good watchdogs.

We drive into the yard. Heat wriggles
over the gravel and dust,
the crushed and stacked Pontiacs,
the off-white islands of kitchen stoves and washers.
We stop at one island,
untie the freezer and slide it out.
I tell Dad to stand back,
then with gloved hands I
slam down the freezer.
It goes whump. Dust swirls up
and nearly glitters.

The truck lurches toward the gate.
A man in blue coveralls smoking a Camel
steps from the tree shade at the entrance
and heads for the building.
"Jesus Christ," I say. "He was watching
we didn't steal anything."
"Of course," Dad says.
"He deals with every son of a bitch in the world."

*T*HE GREAT DIVIDE

Black and white photograph from 1964.
I'm two years old.
My brothers are holding me spread-eagle
against a state park sign with white lettering.
Bill and Buddy, their four hands
lock around my wrists and ankles.
I'm high astraddle the Great Divide
in Dr. Dentons. If I took a leak,
half would trickle to the Atlantic
and half to the Pacific.

Bill and Buddy mug for the camera.
Bill "the tourist" grins, twelve years old
with horn-rim glasses and a white detective hat
with a zebra band.
Buddy looks his tough eighteen, sunburnt
in a T-shirt,
gash of hair black on his forehead.
He pushes weights in Skip's basement
and dates a waitress.

I may have some details
of this photograph wrong.
But the parts about the midline of the mountains—
and my brothers holding me—and the Atlantic and Pacific
I know are right.

PIG IMAGERY

The sunrise tripples as though on fingertips
across the barnyard. Long shadows shoot
from the pockmarks my hooves made.
I expect the tractor's bulk to talk.
Instead, bedsprings harumph. The earth is fat.

My tusks I keep secret
and smoldering like a nun's nightmare,
but today I will menace any fence,
uproot prize tulips, terrorize
whoever is too charitable.

I will float home, and place
the flat of my snout on my parents' house,
the wood lukewarm in the late afternoon,
white, rough.

THE SECRET OF TRAVELING LIGHT

The secret's to be some kind of disciple
for about half an hour. Then have coffee
and debunk your master until the half cup
is cold. There may be something to read

in the dregs, something about doors. In your mind
you stride through a knee-high blaze of newspapers.
You're so lonely you'd kiss a keyhole. You're so hopeful
you'd rescue a tadpole from a Big Daddy bass.

WELCOME TO BIG WYOMING

Interstate 80 hums calm and blue; the Wyoming twilight
lowers its dome. Indian summer. Two stars shoot
toward a rushing pickup, where Bob's awash with wind, but they
   wink out
before the showdown. Roadside sheep double as shrubs.

Bob'll never conquer a Brahman or shout howdy
at a cowed waitress: the sky reminds him of his mildness
and how odd he felt the first time a girl slow-kissed
the acned empire of his homesick face.

SHORELINES

We strummed each other and pleasure bred
in waves of flesh, and a glum goldfish
observed from a shelf. Then I was more girl
than the girl beside me. I was happy.
I wondered about her. I felt like a farmer
made king of a country where cornfields sigh
like expanses of sand. She was no seashell
but I held her and listened: the wishing wells wished.

UNDER A TURQUOISE PORCH LIGHT

A skinny-wristed boy and a fuchsia-pensive girl
fumble a scene as intricate
as a cricket in a crevice: they are trying
to unkindle their tentative love.

North and south of town they'll bathe away
the hours and veils, and the word *love*
may glide through their hollows
like a white hawk on the hunt. Then the word

love may call, ridiculous, in a receding spiral
like a manhole cover wobbled on concrete.
For now the two linger wild as tendrils
between a jar of turquoise gin and a jar of turquoise water.

PET RABBIT SET FREE

Where the suburbs turn to woods a girl
spies a volleyball, between bare trees, deflated,
near sundown. It glows. The girl squints.
Could it be the white rabbit she set free
last spring (Easter present she got tired of)?
A storybook rebirth occurs in her head:
pet rabbit bounding away, radiant,
but the ball, flat, stays put.

The rabbit lasted about a week. Pneumonia.
Pink eyes all filmy, each breath a raw
burble in bronchial tubes, both lungs
become guacamole. Picture the death
from a helicopter: the same off-white oval
(nondescript) as the girl's face peering skyward.

*T*HE SILENCE AND NOISE OF ADOLESCENCE

Out of boredom and a bad report card,
a boy fires a BB into a bird.
A tuft of down hangs in midair,
then dissipates like a dandelion wish.
One scraggle catches in a spiderweb.

But the BB itself—almost a cannonball
on a chickadee's scale of things—
sounds like someone spitting when it
tears through feathers: patoo, this doom
means nothing to me. The empty branch

burns green as ever. Self-absorbed,
the boy likes noise or silence: no talk.
Next day at school, a chalk dust poof
makes the pink linings of his nostrils
itch itch. To disrupt class he sneezes
extra loud and his pal smirks approval.

*H*ORNED TOAD AT THE GRAND CANYON

A family of three rockets cross-country
in a station wagon, eager to elbow
other tourists, to eye-in the abyss
below the Grand Canyon's rim.
They troop out onto a metal platform. The view
evokes *ah, ooh:* obligatory, their sense of beauty.

On the way back to the car, the boy
finds a tiny horned toad and picks it up, somewhat
tweaking its guts between finger and thumb.
The thing turns demonic, hissing, forces
a spurt of purple blood
right out of its eye. The boy flings it

into the brush and hustles ahead, breathless,
to Mom and Pop's tribal comfort, having beheld
the great pagan god of Unexpectedness.
Adrenalin renders his thoughts a mishmash,
but I bet he is thankful: life offers
thrills, beyond public safety, chain link fences.

INTUITION

I

The U.S. of A. with the Grand Coulee Dam
waylaid a whole huge river to serve
her citizens. Blueprints unrolled just right
but people stumble: one heatstroke victim

(salaried or hourly wage, this was one moment)
pinwheeled down the incomplete dam. His face
underwater grew small as a dime. Nevertheless,
turbines whirled. Elsewhere, lights went on.

It reads like one of those tall tales
with Mike Fink or Pecos Bill, this accomplishment,
in pamphlets at the Tourist Center. A large
head of FDR stares into the distance.

II

What I like to look at is the little
town built for workers' families: two rows
of neat houses, a box for a post office,
main street shaded by muscleroot trees,

lawns impossibly green. All around is desert
where mirages wave, shallow; rock sizzles
(or else, collective hiss of rattlesnakes).
Odd to hear sprinklers chikkity-chik,

to see the dam baked ageless, dry on one side.
The sun whams human temples numb.
Surely most teenagers can't wait to leave
this hometown of automatons for college.

III

Come fall, maybe one grade school child will let
the dam overwhelm her daydreams. Maybe
she'll wonder if the fish living by it
in the black water do adapt, evolve,

become their own lights. It's like that
in a limited town: the mind must sense
alternatives. The child will stand with others
(including class bully, future wife-beater,

and one best friend—both created equal?)
and pledge allegiance to a piece of cloth.
Below, the first blind fish will bump
the dam, but find by feel a snail, and eat.

STEPHANIE

She sways on the dance floor. Far back
in the black center of her eyes a spider
builds safety nets in a set of rain barrels
and hums a hex against men. One

of the Replacements, Paul, deadpans
then pleads into his mike
the song "Androgynous." In a forge of backlighting
he shakes off sweat that looks to her like sparks.

Earlier, as she catnapped to a radio's static mutter,
a spider bit into the rose
tattoo on her shoulder, the reddest edge
of the innermost petal. Now it's turning

deeper red. Stephanie's sure of more and less.

PROPHETIC

This desert sun stew-a-brain could start
a prophet's career of tirades, towns,
but I have a private complaint
(Dead ahead the Interstate narrows to a dot):

My traveling companion, a woman, and I
have turned petty in the heat.
Today we debated: was it a vulture
above us, scanning for roadkill,

or a hawk, an eagle? It was nothing,
our argument, yet I stubbornly prop
my arm out the car for maximum
scorch. At times I like being forged

into someone untouchable. Regardless,
burnt skin sings when it hits cool sheets,
hisses even, nonglandular, at peace.
It will be possible, once again, to believe in God.

*F*LIRT

Picture a butterfly balanced on a pith helmet
that sits on quicksand, the struggler gone
under (lungloads of oatmeal, no oxygen):
so lyrical nature and agony man coexist.

Let the butterfly be a certain enticing gesture
impossible to forget: bra strap fidget
on a first date, eye contact maintained
as an abacus clacks countless, long kiss expected.

Let the quicksand be the grave, patient
for every one of us, a succulent mouth
muttering the truth: death, death. What do we get
meanwhile? Lies and lays, moments only.

GOODWILL SWIRLS UP IN THUMBPOOLS

People speak and skirt the sad circles, the campfire halos,
prowl the perimeters and make small jokes. We have to.
We hint at our mythologies so no grown-up
will drown in the dreaminess of a thumbprint.
Thumbprints are pools, and the waters unwind
and converge underground. I'm not complaining. I like
most people. I mean even if one senses the cargo
in his chest, the torrents of doom clouds and daybreaks,
it's hard to talk. Sometimes irony won't do:
the levels of meaning go flat as beer in a plastic cup.
The trick is to be original (like a goggle-eyed virgin
in an emerald mine) but understood (like a hopfrog heart).
At night we sleep in a well and sing for whomever we've lost.

KNIGHT BATTLES BEEHIVE

From a corner of a curl-edge map
rides a knight who hopes
to skewer in battle a dragon's belly.
God, it gets boring. He clanks along,
questioning peasants, squinting over them,
their fields, for telltale scorch marks.

Eyestrain, sore bones ensue. Before long,
his altruistic motives shrink down
to dreams of revenge, which always
simplify: sky entirely blotted out,
then—the dragon killed—clear again.
In the forest, meantime, his horse's hoof

sinks into a soft mound, a beehive. Everything
does disappear. Toppling, his visor vents plugged
with wads of bees, the knight sees nothing.
Who had thought to dodge a river of fire
shot from a dragon snout, finds his head inside a furnace,
his helmet, which magnifies the multi-buzz.

Later, he bathes in a stream, and leaves
his armor standing upright, to rust. Bent lance
laughable now. Quest for glory? Fade to black.

To this day ideals can be limiting. When bee stings
or trivia make me feel trapped, I know
I need water too, a flowing tenderness:
fingers, toes, tongue along an ear's terrain.
Since the only dragon is the fact of death,
glory means: application of mild salve.

STORY

There are days I have no family tree.

No fairy tales, no green riffs to get me through,
just a headache from speculation's

ingrown halo, a pair of sore feet, and high
in bare oak branches a fog that looks

white-hot because it's got
the sun as hostage. Walking

back to work from lunch
I duck into a drugstore: in the aspirin aisle

a withered woman has the air
of a fisherman who's lost

a keeper, a mackerel flashing away
from the visible bait

and invisible line. Let her turn
and tell me, closing her eyes with pleasure,

our long lives are part of a legend.

SLENDER, ALERT, AND ALMOND-EYED THE ALIENS

Slender, alert, and almond-eyed, invisible
to everyone in this city park, the aliens move
among us (I believe). They pick lint from our clothing
with infinite care. It doesn't quite go unnoticed:
we lift our chins. Our faces take
the lunch hour sun full force. Good enough.
The aliens leave without their spacecraft
making a wake, not one sigh from this park
to prove we were touched.

So much for sensitivity: a kid smacks his head
on a teeter-totter. Blood wells up sticky from his scalp
as he yells for his ma, who comes running
to comfort him. She'll take care of him
and pretty quick she'll make sure Frankenstein stitches
are cinched into place. The rest of us lose interest.
(For the second time today I feel at peace.)
A woman on the grass, gazing up at nothing,
rubs her dog's belly, red dick and all.

PLUMBING'S UNDERWORLD

Ultimately a plumber came and exposed them:
they were a family of furtive opulence.
They used too much toilet paper, clogging
pipes, and dropped bobby pins down drains
with impunity, also poured bacon grease, which
turned to fat nearly as gruesome
as table scraps from cannibals. And
Crystal Drāno had only made matters worse.

The plumber grunted, noncommittal, kept at the mess.
The father stood by with hands at his sides.
The mother breast-fed the baby in a back room.
What else could they do? The plumber had tools,
also self-confidence toward the underworld.
He worked until the sinks again emptied quickly
and the tub didn't gurgle when the toilet flushed.
Then they all had coffee. The men shook hands.

Maybe, after imaginary sins and a sense of relief,
the family believed they were a lot like their neighbors.
The spearmint patch, green sparks above the septic tank,
gave them some joy, despite the grave odor.

WHEN I SUBMERGE ALMOST MY WHOLE HEAD

When I submerge almost my whole head
in the bathtub, my face afloat with eyes closed,
I hear a roaring like a hurricane hustling
torrential glory straight toward me.

Toward my face, an island in repose.
Toward my knees, monoliths winglike, smooth
kin to pyramids, and pinnacles of leisure
for cormorants and pearl divers.

I open my eyes. I'd like my skin to prickle
to indicate panic among the natives—forget
the storm, the island itself
come to life—but nothing happens.

I raise my ears above the waterline.
Instead of a hurricane I hear
the irregular rattle-tap of rain on tin
somewhere in the attic, as though a rat

rocked back and forth an empty cup.

My toes shall tower

My big toes, like dropped clocks, look lopsided.
My long ones can crook like a witch's fingers:
when I flex them, they beckon
to Hansel and Gretel. My little ones
are afterthoughts, eyes sprouted from muddy spuds.
They're all as blunt as gargoyle tongues.

I've had enough, though, of hairy toes,
baroque knuckles. Tonight it's good-bye to grotesque.

Tonight my toes shall tower
above blankets and sheets, or appear to tower,
shadow-sculpted, a miniature Stonehenge
of my flesh. Then I'll possess
a warm place of worship, a child's way
to count the round hours.

HOUSE ON FIRE

I've been civilized by the idea of time
but made wild by what? Not by the roar
of a rose, but by a howl like a hatchet

flung from this planet. By a house on fire.
By a soul hurled from a framework. By a hillside aswim
with heat wraiths and shadows, really bruises

which move. By ashes. By a wedding ring
fused to what's left. By principles
in a wilderness where I go watchful.

*T*HE SEVEN RIVERS OF HIROSHIMA

On a porch in Georgia
an old man and his hounds, still drunk
with last night's hunting, slept in a layered
settlement of themselves. A copperhead
blended into the kudzu and flowed closer.
Sunday morning: the heathens fleshed out faith
in cyclical business, intimate life.
In Hiroshima
a regiment of men with ruined eyes
called for water, and seven rivers
spread their stories to the rest of the world.

HARBORVIEW MEDICAL CENTER

. . . .

Since his brain surgery my father
is wander-eyed and soft-spoken, his head
rolled toward me on a Harborview pillow.
I make small talk, tell how I sprinkled flour

around the water bowl on our back porch
and after dark the flour was frailly etched
with raccoon tracks, a few mice whispers.
My father never prayed in his life.

That bowl of water keeps the clear eye
of itself as it evaporates, indifferent
to all, rereturning to states of rain.
The surgeons say he'll be himself again.

TADPOLES

Under my gaze they began back legs,
the tadpoles my father helped me capture
and carry home in a lanternlike jar
of cloudy water. I didn't know what work
their lives were. One day they all went

belly up and were done becoming
the overseers, metal-irised, of dry ditches.
My father poured them into the toilet.
In the water-spiral their bodies blurred,
regaining tails. A sliver tingled in my left sole.

I would never be tall or decisive.
I would stand in doorways, easily entranced.

*I*N THE BARN

. . . .

A cat composed as an uncut pie
sits on a rope-chafed rafter
and watches a boy, about fourteen, in overalls
apply mascara. What kind of future
can a boy like that have?
What useful work will he ever do?
He lies back on unbaled hay, his features lit
with a picture he saw in a magazine.
The cat blinks six times quick
seeing him come.
Then the cat climbs down
and licks his hand. Observer and introvert:
how they beg to be devoured.

Skagit Valley, 1980

Long after my last drop of adrenalin
has been diluted, I remember three young men, rural
Anyburg. Bored, we drove the back roads fast.
Beer cans clattered. Tires squealing, we took the curves.
I could not forget Nastassia Kinski's lips

fleshing out the flat drive-in screen: real life.
(Not one of us had ever had sex or held a job.)
Maybe all we wanted was a woman with legs spread
in a wheelbarrow of twenty dollar bills, and beer foam
falling from the sky: life should be so easy. We knew

little about domination: the brutality hinted at
by the staples stuck in the centerfold's belly, or
the way a time clock bites down to set the pay.
We submitted to standard dreams. We believed
the mass media run by big men bragging. But

we had some cunning, too: we built up the forces
in the bunkers of our tear ducts, and didn't talk much.

*L*ITTLE ROOM, RETARDED HEART

Tonight nothing touches him, not even the naked women
and cheeseburgers drawn with charcoal on butcher paper
(such are the friezes of his old attic room).
He is visiting his parents. He is getting sleepy:

greasy burgers on a hot grill. He used to love
to sit in diners late at night, nearly convinced
he was wild. The waitress (no wedding ring) was all smiles.
The fry cook flipped a patty. It seared louder.

A loner tucked a dollar bill under his saucer
and left looking hard at scuffed wingtips.
A pair of cops talked low, murmured into coffee cups.
At so lonesome an hour these men seemed noble,

concerned with other than a full stomach
and sex sex sex. Back then he envied them
their world weariness and their private
business, their rooms blank like this one.

WHEN A HONEYBEE UNFREEZES FROM A FLOWER HEAD

. . . .

A skein of fog is caught on fir needles,
a rigor mortis goldfinch hangs downside up
from a twig: a man squats naked atop
a stump, anus aimed at its inmost ring.

The man would feel as old as the trees
and be forgiving, his beard grow in
as soft as moss. But who doesn't learn
from pain alone? When a honeybee unfreezes

from a flower head, the man starts thinking
again. He's scared where he might get stung.
Greedy for safety, remembering everyself,
he gets dressed and goes away.

*P*UDDLE OF CATSUP, PARSLEY SPRIG

The red-haired man would (per usual) pinch
the waitress, except his wife leans close
in the cafe booth. Glasses of water sweat cold.
A zigzag vein at the man's temple thumps.

His world is getting blurry, both eyes white
with cataracts, but the hospital spooks him.
He pictures a razor slitting runny yolks
and it causes his balls to pull up.

His wife is persistent. Again she urges him
in a whisper: "Honey, it needs to be done."
How powerless he feels, puny, a passenger
of events: a frozen pea rides an ice floe.

Her world is perfect. She tells herself
she feels true pity. By ignoring infidelities
she becomes a kind of Admiral Byrd, conquering petty
matters, claiming she loves her husband. But

man and wife, both, are snowblind.

Look at that cigarette stubbed out
in a puddle of catsup, by a parsley sprig
an unreal green. Look at that waitress
when she turns away: she hates them.

BETWEEN BEING STUPID AND ACTIVELY CRUEL

Lies between being stupid and actively cruel
a sloggy field you must cross by trudging
alone, noticing graves which stoic children
have dug their pets: canaries buried in cigar boxes,
dogs and cats wrapped tight in security blankets.

The graves make you laugh the more you leave behind
your lean-to in the woods (i.e. stupidity), the closer
you approach the amusement park (active cruelty, of course).
The furious cuckold in charge of the Ferris wheel
has stranded his wife, terrified of heights, at the very

top: coaxing and sobbing, deep wild pleading. It's hilarious.
You laugh so hard your tears burn with the rides' neon.
When you arrive, you will tickle into submission
the first girl you ever loved, and never slept with.

Who the fuck did she think she was,
leading you on and not coming across?
You will tickle her till she laughs and cries.
You will enjoy her contortions in the Hall of Mirrors.

Maybe you figure conflicting emotions make one an adult.
Guess again, in the field of dead pets: real grief is simple.

WELL-BEING

(A balsa wood glider once wheeled and nosedived
down an open well, rested on water: lost, for good.)
My friend slings on a white sportscoat,
ties a paisley silk tie, sidewalk-flying

to his workplace. We blurt good-byes,
having talked about clothing. We had lunch
at a Denny's, a waitress named Bobbi.
Summer smog hung outside, burning vaguely.

Now my friend disappears (flash) into
a building, revolving glass doors, express elevator.
Rushing elsewhere, everyone ferocious, it seems always
we order food and then (fast) get on with it.

Some swallowing is gentler. I have held ten mice
cupped in my hands, newborns, hairless, their mother's milk
visible inside them: plumps of white bellywarmth,
wriggling everyway. Some swallowing is gentler

yet, perfectly still. I have cradled
a face, my penis gone soft in her mouth.
(Oh, I love underground, vertigo, cool
smell of algae to welcome me home.)

ANTI-MANNEQUIN

A mannequin could bob content in freezing water,
as the *Titanic*'s lost assuredly did not.
Nothing bugs a mannequin. I witnessed one (nude)
tucked under someone's arm and carried across
a city street, its crotch bald, featureless, entire
body hard. Maybe that's the state which military
fiends aspire to: self-contained, not a bit frail.

I favor a pinch of fat, a greenstick fracture,
indigestion, an active tongue, a groan to answer
the alarm clock squalling. It's not possible to perfect
a self. Most adults (post-dreaming) become children
again, led to cubicles, bland lunches in boxes,
days of tedium and fitting in, busted crayons,
dead-end jobs. I thought adulthood meant autonomy.

What happens, after all? Is justice done daily in hell
and heaven? Maybe my vital juices will be slurped
up by a tree's taproot, and I will live on
in the leaves, benevolent. I like that idea.
Will I lose consciousness? I don't know. For now, I say
let the wind have its way with my four limbs,
tangling mine with others, disengaging, on and on.
I say God bless momentum, God bless the gone.

DUCKERT THE EFFEMINATE, ZEPHYRLIKE SURGEON

I

A kind of resurrection, a real mess, a side of beef
heaves by on a hook. It's business as usual
at a meat-packing plant: red floor slime, some human

blood. Conveyor belts bear off steaks, finger parts,
all possible succulents, as one. Choppers and buzz saws
provide oblivion, white noise, but outside it's animal

calm, the stench of stockyards. At dawn pink clouds
preside over cud-chewing. Once I drove through
Sioux Falls, South Dakota, and held my nose.

II

Duckert breezes into the exam room, long white coat
a wake of cologne. Briefly, the nurse flirts.
Duckert wants to "debulk" the tumor in my dad's neck.

He explains the risks, tells us the facts: "best chance
for long-term survival." Then the decision is
out of his hands: fingers as fine as cricket

cage bars, cuticles perfect like hummingbird hymens.
He is precise, the room air-conditioned. Silk socks
encase his ballerina's ankles: sheer purple.

III

Is Duckert more like a worker in a meat-packing plant
or my old self, holding its nose, wishing elsewhere?
He is the worst of both, I think: brutal, aloof.

· · ·

I can see him scrubbing up and putting on his pale
green mask. It goes in and out (slow breath, slow
breath) as the scalpel descends toward the dotted line.

He prolongs the delicate moment (clothes neatly folded
in the next room, Rolex ticking in the toe of a shoe).
Then he slices. Then he comes to life.

*H*OSPITAL SIDEWALK

In this hospital they itemize the cost
of a person's deathbed down to the last aspirin.
They charge twenty-five dollars for fake lamb's wool
on which, after surgery, patients bleed.
People die with eyes fixed on digital clocks
which flip numbers every minute, dollar signs flying.

The sidewalk out front has blades of grass
shooting up through cracks. A ladybug
(not much bigger than a decimal point) could climb
to the highest tip and fly away home
to save her children. I wonder if little things comfort
anyone. Not me. The business of love is living big.

FROG

Maybe a lawn sprinkler on late played Siren
to his pinhole ears. Anyhow, the frog left
the pond. Headlight-swept, he crossed a road.
My car passed over him but I could see

in the rearview mirror he was okay.
Then again, is a thing so soft ever safe?
Leaping, he flailed webfeet. How green the lawn,
how heavy the smell from where there's water.

I drove on to sit by a bed in Intensive Care,
where my father slept among machines. As if grateful
for wet grass, the frog wept with all his skin,
so happy, so helpless: not dead, not dead.

MY MOTHER'S MOUTH

Her lower lip has been left numb
by a stroke. It can't detect a crumb,
and her hands are so weak they can't
turn off hard enough the bath faucet.

At night the house fills with a sound
as of crying. Really, it's water: drip
and trickle it travels seaward, toward
plankton and sunlight, key to all life—

an octopus, attacked, raves black and red and
more sharks cruise in to thrust for scraps.
There is the world: devouring, clouded.
Here, my mother's mouth: half-devoured.

GLINT OF GOLD TOOTH IN A POORLY LIT KITCHEN

My father in a broth-stained undershirt
as he laughs weary in our weak-light kitchen

sounds like a mouse running—raspy chuckle,
fear scurry, grain of rice seized and bitten.

How small one life is, and how tightly
we hold on to it. But cancer (for example)

can grab life back, knot up a tumor fist
unremoveable. What then must a person do?

Live smaller and smaller. Wash a bowl
as my father does, with a motion as of

panning for gold, glint in his mouth
as he peers down—not smiling, not grimacing—

into the water, dimmer and dimmer, knives at the bottom.

DESTINATION: PLANET OVUM

Age ten I found out my parents had sex
for fun. I walked in on white skin.
She laughed; he did not. A sweat film caul
swept across my face. Who were these people?

The ones who said "fuck" was an ugly word.
They were "making love." They were making noise!
What a little boy I was, feeling betrayed.
The other night I saw my father in boxer shorts:

my palest future, with hairless legs. A person
loses everything, illusions first, torn
in hospitals, honeycombs of hurting bodies
and pure white sheets. When I get sick

of this world, I think about sperm.
A man manufactures an endless supply, billions
of spaceships with a dream destination: Planet Ovum.
In other words a baby could be anyone.

SUNDAY HARDWARE STORE

If a butt-biting midget ran amuck,
we customers would cease our milling.
People would yip and curse and—midget
vanished up a heating vent—then be silent.

What precedent would there be?
Maybe the pure-alive alertness
astronauts feel strong at blast-off
(G-forces tussle their faces).

Instead, fluorescent tubes above us
fiercely buzz: so the mundane
asserts itself. I stand in line
with potting soil, and watch one black hair

on a clerk turn white, the way a star streaks
when it falls, burning, a small occurrence.
There is no other world for us.
Mousetraps, bug spray, preserve our safety.

GALAPAGOS ISLANDS, GUILLOTINE EYELIDS

Iguanas grabble on Galapagos rocks
in a *National Geographic* movie.
A teenage boy naps in the last row
of the classroom. He's not popular, a nobody.

He wakes up to find a single iguana's
face filling the screen, a stare hypnotic
with one quick blink. The boy
is thrilled, thinks to himself: *so cold-blooded.*

Alert in every nerve, he cannot return
to dreaming. Across the room the object
of his desires, a girl with black hair,
leans forward and reveals her neck.

It gleams. Why be lonely, lucid, keen,
eyelids like a guillotine, heart a walnut?
She looks at him. He looks to the screen.
As if by a falling blade, again, the boy is lost:

closing his eyes he sees Gary Cooper, a lone gun,
a good man. Then the boy replays a porno film, paid for
a quarter at a time, bad milk spilled in a booth.
What sort of man will he be? Opening his eyes

he sees lizards lash tails in the surf, writhing,
mouths full of algae, and not so grotesque, really.
In fact, they look happy. The girl smiles at him.
He is afraid to smile back. But, desiring his life, he does.